1.Introduction

Being sick,probably the worst time ever is where this story starts,in a room that looks like a scientists lab.Because of all the robots,test tubes,crystals,liquids and books,lots of books ranging from chemistry to technology.In there is a bed belonging to a sickly boy with poor eyesight named Myth,who is accompanied with one of the most popular internet stars called Star.Star and Myth are best friends and today Myth had an accident where him and Star, were watching cat videos when he laughed to hard he fell out of the window and landed into a pollen farm where his cheeks plumped up kinda looking like a squirrel with nuts in its cheeks.

Now in his room there playing nuts and bolts which is a knockoff version of chess.While he was about to call technology Star was brainstorming ideas of where to go because she wanted to go on a trip.First she thought of the space centre but then she thought of a better idea."Let's go to the Green House!"Star shouted, trying to add happiness to make Myth go."Absolutely not" Myth said trying to imitate his dad's voice."You can just go to the cactus bit" Star said making sure not to be sarcastic."Ok,I guess so" Myth said. "OMG,yes," Star said.

The next morning,Star rushed out of bed taking her morning selfie of course.Two doors away,Myth was lying in bed with a terrible headache from the fall last night.Just then Myst got a text from star saying "i'm coming now" at that moment Myth got ready as fast as he could.Right when Star knocked, Myth bolted to the door as fast as a cheetah trying not to trip.When he got to the door he saw a giant sparkly star that was attached to a rope.Immediately he knew it was Star so he greeted her with their signature handshake."OMGs,i'm so excited are you"Star said.

"I'm very"replied Myth trying to hide the fact he was scared.After they had lunch,The friends

walked to the greenhouse with Star adding little whistles for each step."Are you a little bit scared"coward Myth
."No,why you ask?"replied Star."No reason,"Myth said in a sweet tone.
"Good,then let's hurry"Star said

2.Prickily Grass Monster

When they got there they first sat down and had their little lunch that was only a cucumber cob and a delicious chocolate cake.After that it turned dark and misty and Myth suggested they should go back to their house and come back tomorrow.But Star had already opened the door and went in so Myth went to go catch her.When Myth got inside it looked like it had turned wider because the room was so big he couldn't see Star.Just then,the doors slammed shut with a big vine holding the door handles to make sure no one escapes.Myth was shivering in fear scared of what would happen to him when he saw Star getting chased by a prickly grass ball the size of a boulder.

In a split second,he went and helped Star but it was no use and now they were both getting chased by a prickly grass ball.While they were getting chased Star saw a cactus and had a brilliant idea.When they went in a circle 3 more times Star picked up the cactus and threw it at the prickly grass ball.Unluckily,it absorbed it and became a giant grass monster and that made the situation even worse.

While almost getting smashed Myth found a door that looked safe.So he grabbed Star and they bolted to the door at the speed of light.

After nearly getting flattened by Star,Myth saw a cylinder that had some words on it that read 'Bug spray'.When they both got up Myth had another look at the bug spray which had a sentence on the back that read 'Can kill plants'. "This is our secret weapon"shouted Myth excitedly."What is"questioned Star."This bug spray,it can kill plants"replied Myth."Cool"said Star.

"But how many squirts does it have?"said Star.Myth shaked it and replied in a sad tone"There's only one"."Then we better make it work"Star said.Then they went out of the room with the bug spray in their hands trying to be as quiet as a mouse.

3.Grass Ashes

Myst was still a bit scared and was trying to be as stealthy as a ninja.But Star was trying to be brave and formidable as a lion trying to get it's prey.Beep!went Star's phone accidentally luring the grass monster to their location."Found you"shouted the grass monster trying to act scary.Straight away the grass monster picked up the two friends and took the bug spray from them.They felt the grass monster's gross and slimy hand nearly losing grip of them.

"Who should I spray this liquid on?" said the grass monster.Just then,the monster sprayed Myth and he turned into a puddle of grass ashes.There he lay as a puddle of ashes on the shiny greenhouse floor.When Star was done crying her eyes out she slipped through the monsters hand and gathered up Myth's ashes,finally running to the science room.When she got there she felt dehydrated so she went to the tap to get some nice cold water.But when she turned the tap a grass snake popped out and spat poison at her.The snake looked fierce with a giant spiked horn that looked like it injected poison into the heart.Luckily,the spit only got her sparkly new shirt that had a star on it.In the distance,she could see a well that looked safe.Without a doubt,she bolted to the well in a flash.

Star fell for a long time while holding the bottle of grass ashes in her hands the best she could.She landed with a thud next to a lake that looked like it was deadly.As she looked around she saw a person in the distance.When she got up she rushed to the mysterious person.But just then she got stopped by a seaweed monster that had a giant grass sword that was poisonous.The seaweed monster quickly swung his sword but luckily Star ducked with immense speed.After about five more swings the seaweed monster fell in the water and dropped his sword on the path.With the sword Star felt more confident and rushed to help the person she saw.Five minutes later,Star got to the person and saw that it was held captured in a honey farm.When Star was about to set free the person some honey mosquitos bit Star in the leg.Blood was running down her leg and she was so worried and wanted revenge.When she felt better she swung her sword at the mosquitos trying not to hit the person. She continuously swung her sword and eventually she hit all of them.When the person was set free she learned that her name was Luna and that she has been stuck here for over 5 years!As Star was about to tell Luna about Myth,Star got eaten by this giant venus flytrap that looked as big as a mountain.Luna was scared and ran for her life not even picking up the grass ashes container.

4.Stomach Bug

Inside the venus flytraps stomach,Star saw that it was as big as a prison cell,so that meant that she had some exploring to do.There was slime everywhere so it took ages to explore but in one little slime puddle she found a book.The title on it was 'Turning ashes into people' which made her happy because that's exactly what she needed.Surprisingly,there was only one page with a recipe on it.The ingredients on it were Venus flytrap teeth,Grass snake horn and grass monster slime.Star knew that getting the teeth was going to be easier than the others so she was determined to get that first.

But Before she could get the Venus flytraps teeth, the flytrap probably felt a bit sick because acid was coming up his tummy.It was moving left and right making Star have to grab on to his tonsil which was very slimy and wet.But luckily from the momentum of the tonsil, she swung of it and landed right on it's tooth.Star climbed it and made sure she didn't touch the bottom because it was very spiky.Luckily, she accidentally broke of a bit of the tooth which made her able to rip some of the the tooth away.After a little bit of work,she finally made the tooth fall out which was done by taking of the top part of the tooth.While dropping she jumped and broke the flytrap jaw.

SPLIT!SPLAT!SPLIT!SPLAT!

She grabbed the tooth and ran taking Luna by her shirt she ran and ran until she found something.She found the toilets and she found a monster having a pee and disgustingly she saw wet green slime.So disgustingly she and

Luna grabbed a plant bowl and scooped it out the toilet which she was thinking was the most disgusting thing in her life.

But now she had ⅔ of the items for the potion to revive Myth so she and Luna ran everywhere trying to find the grass snake in the science room until…

BANG!

The Grass monster crashed into Luna knocking her out and stomping on Star in the process.Star tried to get up and just had the strength to do it but Luna was badly injured and couldn't even get up.But luckily the grass monster didn't notice her so Star ran to the science room cause she remembered she needed to find that snake so she got there and SSSSSS!!! Went the snake but with perfect reactions Star caught the snake then she ripped the horn of the snake scurried away then.STOMP!!!The grass monster stepped so close to Star so Star ran away to where Luna was but Luna was dead.Star cried so much but she had to be strong so she ran back to the science room but the monster was blocking it.Star didn't know what to do but she had an idea so she threw a plant pot in the other room and the monster scuttled to the pot.Star dashed to the science room she found a plant pot and started to make the recipe she stirred and mushed and grinded until it was done.Star poured the what looked like a stew into the ashes then **Bang!!!**Myth appeared again but because of the huge bang it lured the grass monster to their whereabouts.

5.The Finale

With the grass monster approaching Star quickly held Myth and ran but the monster spotted them and quickly scuttled to them.Star and Myth were scared because the grass monster was approaching and it was a dead end.The Grass Monster picked them up and was about to gobble them down until **Bluuurgh!!!**Myth was so scared she spewed onto the grass monster's eye temporarily blinding him so Myth and Star slid through his hands.They ran to the science room going through the monster's leg.They hid behind the table inside the room.Thinking hardly they tried to think of an idea until Myth had one.His idea was that to lure the monster to the door then in the nick of time dodge out the way to break the door to escape.So Star quickly alerted the monster and ran to the door and of course the monster followed so the grass monster scuttles to her.But it looked like Star wasn't moving so quickly like a hero he dived pushing Star out the way.The door smashed open but then the worst day ever happened…